The Night Iguana Left Home

A Richard Jackson Book

The Night Iguana Left Home

by Megan McDonald

pictures by Ponder Goembel

A DK INK BOOK • DK PUBLISHING, INC.

For Cathy Camper, friend with two *n*'s —M.M.

For Allen, who created scrumptious stews while I created Iguana art —P.G.

A Richard Jackson Book

DK
Ink

DK Publishing, Inc., 95 Madison Avenue, New York, New York 10016
Visit us on the World Wide Web at http://www.dk.com

Text copyright © 1999 by Megan McDonald
Illustrations copyright © 1999 by Ponder Goembel

Library of Congress Cataloging-in-Publication Data
McDonald, Megan.
The night Iguana left home / by Megan McDonald ; illustrated by Ponder Goembel. — 1st ed.
p.   cm.
"A Richard Jackson book"
Summary: Although her friend Alison Frogley treats her very well,
Iguana feels that something is missing in her life.
ISBN: 0-7894-2581-5
[1. Iguanas—Fiction. 2. Friendship—Fiction. 3. Contentment—Fiction.]
I. Goembel, Ponder, ill. II. Title.
PZ7.M478419Ni   1999   [E]—dc21   98-7372   CIP   AC

The illustrations for this book were done in sepia ink with watercolor washes.
The text of this book is set in 18 point Nofret.
Printed and bound in USA
First Edition, 1999
2 4 6 8 10 9 7 5 3 1

I guana had a good life at the Frogleys' house. Or so it seemed to Alison Frogley, her friend and almost sister. Iguana had a closet with a heating pad, a free library card, her own e-mail address, and all the anchovy pizza she could eat. Once a day Alison misted her with salt spray from a squeegee bottle. And . . . there were no dogs.

But something was not right with Iguana.

Alison noticed that Iguana's eyes looked watery. Her tail was too thin. Three of her nails were broken. Her dewlap drooped, and her skin was peeling.

"You need more calcium," said Alison. She spoon-fed Iguana vanilla ice cream and strained spinach. They ate from paper plates so Iguana would not have to do the dishes, the chore she hated most.

Iguana sighed. "Do you ever find yourself just wishing for some good old-fashioned sea-weed?" she asked.

"You? Seaweed? I thought you hated sea-weed!" said Alison. She called up the sushi restaurant and ordered one dozen California rolls wrapped in extra seaweed. Iguana barely touched them.

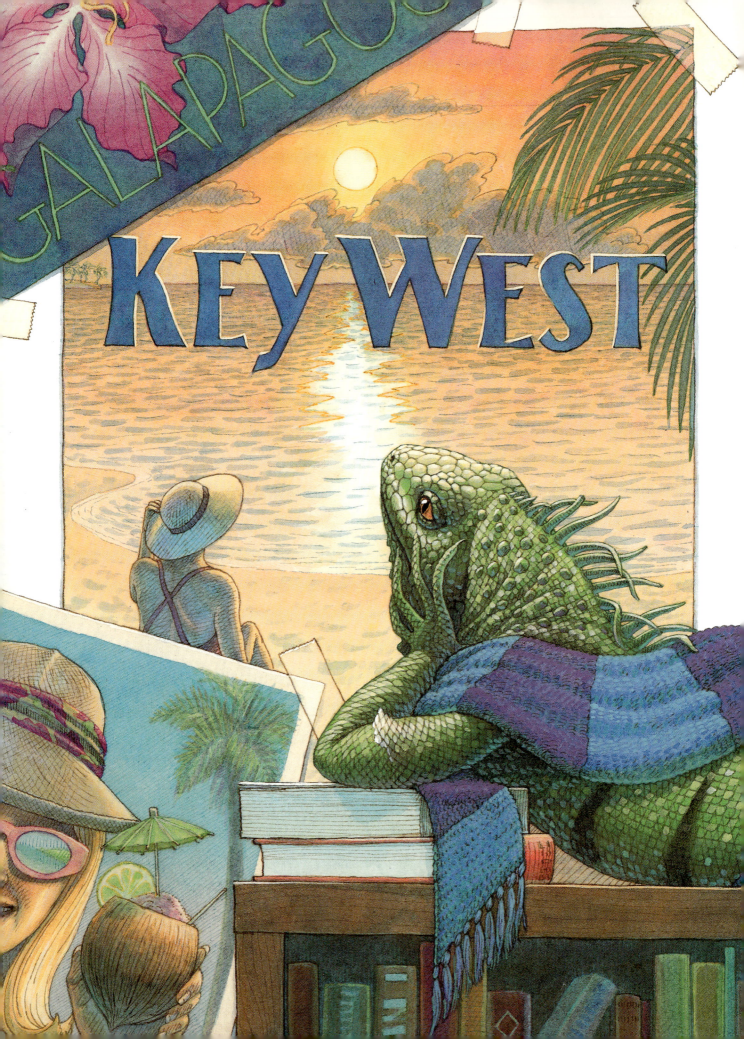

KEY WEST

GALAPAGOS

Something was still not right with Iguana.

Iguana perched on top of Alison's bookcase and stared at the travel posters papering her walls. JAMAICA, FIJI, THE GALAPAGOS ISLANDS. An island getaway might be the ticket, but she didn't have a passport. KEY WEST. Florida! No passport necessary! But there was still her fear of flying. She crawled downstairs.

Visit The Fiji Islands

The idea came to her while watching educational television. Her favorite TV star, Liz, rode to the bottom of the ocean with a wacky teacher in—of all things—a bus.

A bus!

Iguana woke up the next morning and added an *n* to her name. *Iguanna*, she scrawled, in cursive, in the steam on the bathroom mirror. Then she kissed it.

She packed her bathing suit, library books, and plenty of suntan lotion. She stuck her free pizza coupon on Alison's mirror. Then Iguana spiked her hair and pointed her tail south.

At the bus station, she bought a ticket, one way, to Key West, and rode a bus with a big dog on it that wasn't real. No problem. "Good-bye, heating pad. Hello, sunshine!" she said.

Iguana squinted in the bright light as she stepped off the bus. She purchased a Panama hat, sunglasses, and a picture postcard, which she addressed to Alison Frogley.  She licked the stamp twice, it tasted so good. I hope she knows it's from me, thought Iguana.

Back in Schenectady, Alison sadly taped Iguana's postcard, palm trees out, to her mirror, right next to the free pizza coupon, which she would never, ever use.

For a short time, Iguana lived the high life, just like Liz, the TV star. By day, she swam and surfed in the ocean.  At night, she discovered a whole new world—dining out. She ate snails and caviar, papaya and mustard greens, hibiscus flowers. And gravel for dessert.

Soon her allowance was gone. She tried to call Alison collect, but nobody was home at the Frogleys'.

Iguana's sunburn itched. Her library books were overdue. And the seaweed tasted like cardboard. She addressed a mosquito postcard to Alison. Not even the taste of the stamp cheered her up.

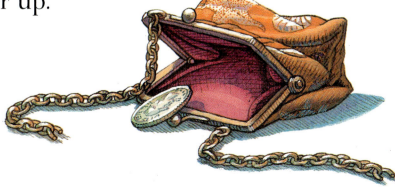

Just when Iguana thought her luck had run out, she noticed a sign in a restaurant window for a job. HELP WANTED. She filled out an application.

"You wash dishes?" the man asked.

"In the dishes I wash, you can see yourself!" said Iguana.

"Do you like dogs?"

Iguana almost choked with terror. But she needed the money.

"They like *me*!" she told the man.

"Good! Call me Archie."

Iguana washed dishes till her thumbs wrinkled. When Archie's dog, Bruno, came near, Iguana whipped her tail around to scare him.

Then came Festival Night. Iguana had never seen so many dirty dishes! The cook made his once-a-year specialty: *gallina de palo*. Translation: iguana stew! But Iguana did not read Spanish. The stew looked like plain old chicken to her. It even smelled like chicken.

By eight o'clock, they had run out of the special.

"What are we going to do?" asked Archie.

"All we need is one fat female," said the cook. He squinted at Iguana. Archie took off his glasses and peered at her strangely.

"What's so special about this special, anyway?" Iguana asked. "It's chicken, right?" Archie and the cook laughed.

She looked up at the board. GALLINA DE PALO—BEST IGUANA STEW IN THE KEYS.

Gallina de Palo—
Best Iguana
stew in the
Keys

Iguana dropped
the plate she was washing.
She was so upset she spread her dewlap.

"Look at that. She has a throat pouch!" said
Archie. "Get her!"

Iguana raced out the back door and across
the sand, heading for water, Bruno only a bus
length behind. She let go her tail, then dived in.
Iguana swam like a snake, holding her breath
underwater for half an hour, until she surfaced
on No Name Key, next to Big Pine.

 In Schenectady, Alison Frogley missed her friend Iguana. She tried calling the restaurant where Iguana worked. They said she left one day in a hurry. No forwarding address.

In no time, Iguana's spiked hair went limp. She lost her sunglasses. She frequented a large Dumpster behind the pizza parlor. She missed Alison, but she had no money for bus fare. Then one day as she dragged her tail down Main Street on Big Pine, an idea hit her. Her best yet.

There she was in front of the post office! Iguana climbed right up on the counter and volunteered to lick a few stamps. She licked sixty stamps a minute. "Hired!" said the woman in the blue shirt.

Two days later, Alison Frogley received a mysterious package on her doorstep, postmarked Big Pine, Florida. "Iguana!" Alison screeched when she opened the box, and they hugged hard until neither one could breathe. The two friends ordered anchovy pizza and stuffed themselves silly.

FRAGILE

To: Alison Frogley
Schenectady N.Y.

Iguana stayed in Schenectady until her skin began to peel. Alison rubbed Iguana's head and misted her with salt spray, but she knew it was time for her friend to leave for the warm South. So Alison lined Iguana's box with glossy scenes from magazines, propped up her head on the heart–shaped pillow she had embroidered with *Iguanna* in fancy letters, and shipped her priority mail back to Big Pine Key.

In just a few short weeks, Iguana had her own room with two PBS channels, a photo I.D. library card, her own e–mail address, and a job she was good at—licking stamps at the Big Pine post office. She could be seen basking in the sun on weekends, looking rather well at six–and–a–half feet and weighing twenty–nine pounds.

Iguana e–mailed Alison at least three times a week and faithfully sent her a genuine hand–written–in–cursive letter every Sunday. Twice a year, she mailed herself back to Schenectady in a very long box, where she and her true friend, Alison Frogley, shared the best anchovy pizza in the whole world.